THE TAN CAN

All inquiries should be addressed to:
Barron's Educational Series, Inc.
250 Wireless Boulevard
Hauppauge, NY 11788

International Standard Book Number 0-8120-4856-3

Library of Congress Catalog Card Number 91-41675

Library of Congress Cataloging-in-Publication Data

Foster, Kelli C.
   The tan can / by Foster & Erickson; illustrations by Kerri Gifford.
   p. cm. (Get ready—get set—read!)
   Summary: A rhinoceros, crab, monkey, and bird join forces to
open a can they find in the sand.
ISBN 0-8120-4856-3
   (1. Animals—Fiction.   2. Containers—Fiction.   3. Stories in rhyme.)
I. Erickson, Gina Clegg. II. Russell, Kerri Gifford, ill. III. Title. IV. Series:
Erickson, Gina Clegg. Get ready—get set—read!
PZ8.3.T1445 1992
(E)—dc20   91-41675
                                                                          CIP
                                                                          AC

PRINTED IN HONG KONG
6 7 8 9 0   9927   11 10 9 8 7 6

GET READY...GET SET...READ!

THE TAN CAN

by
Foster & Erickson

Illustrations by
Kerri Gifford Russell

BARRON'S

The small band

ran on the sand.

Stan found a
brand new can.

Who can open it?

"I can," said Nan,
and she began.

But Nan could not open
the sandy can.

"I can," said Dan,
and he tries his hand.

But Dan could not open
the dandy can.

"I can," said Jan,
and away she ran.

But Jan could not open
the tan can.

"I have a plan,"
said Nan.

"*We* can open
the brand new,
sandy, dandy, tan can!"

Up go Jan and Nan.

Nan lets go of the can.

It lands on Stan!

The End

The AN Word Family

began	Nan
can	plan
Dan	ran
Jan	Stan

The AND Word Family

and	hand
band	lands
brand	sand
dandy	sandy

Sight Words

his
new
who
away
have
open
could
found
small
tries

Dear Parents and Educators:

Welcome to *Get Ready...Get Set...Read!*

We've created these books to introduce children to the magic of reading.

Each story in the series is built around one or two word families. For example, *A Mop for Pop* uses the OP word family. Letters and letter blends are added to OP to form words such as TOP, LOP, and STOP. As you can see, once children are able to read OP, it is a simple task for them to read the entire word family. In addition to word families, we have used a limited number of "sight words." These are words found to occur with high frequency in the books your child will soon be reading. Being able to identify sight words greatly increases reading skill.

You might find the steps outlined on the facing page useful in guiding your work with your beginning reader.

We had great fun creating these books, and great pleasure sharing them with our children. We hope *Get Ready...Get Set...Read!* helps make this first step in reading fun for you and your new reader.

Kelli C. Foster, PhD
Educational Psychologist

Gina Clegg Erickson, MA
Reading Specialist

Guidelines for Using *Get Ready...Get Set...Read!*

Step 1.   Read the story to your child.

Step 2.   Have your child read the Word Family list aloud several times.

Step 3.   Invent new words for the list. Print each new combination for your child to read. Remember, nonsense words can be used (*dat, kat, gat*).

Step 4.   Read the story *with* your child. He or she reads all of the Word Family words; you read the rest.

Step 5.   Have your child read the Sight Word list aloud several times.

Step 6.   Read the story *with* your child again. This time he or she reads the words from both lists; you read the rest.

Step 7.   Your child reads the entire book to you!

There are five sets of books in the

Series. Each set consists of five **FIRST BOOKS**
and two **BRING-IT-ALL-TOGETHER BOOKS**.

SET 1

is the first set your children should read.
The word families are selected from the short vowel sounds:
at, **ed**, **ish** and **im**, **op**, **ug**.

SET 2

provides more practice
with short vowel sounds:
an and **and**, **et**, **ip**, **og**, **ub**.

SET 3

focuses on
long vowel sounds:
ake, **eep**, **ide** and **ine**, **oke** and **ose**, **ue** and **ute**.

SET 4

introduces the idea that the word family sounds
can be spelled two different ways:
ale/ail, **een/ean**, **ight/ite**, **ote/oat**, **oon/une**.

SET 5

acquaints children with word families that
do not follow the rules for long and short vowel sounds:
all, **ound**, **y**, **ow**, **ew**.